D0959178

HELLO! WELCOME TO THE FABUMOUSE WORLD OF THE THEA SISTERS!

Thea Sisters

Hi, I'm Thea Stilton, Geronimo Stilton's sister! I am a special reporter for The Rodent's Gazette, the most famouse newspaper on Mouse Island. I love traveling and meeting new mice all over the world like the Thea Sisters. These five friends have helped me out with my adventures. Let me introduce you to these fabumouse young mice!
Colette has a real passion for fashion. She loves to design her own clothes in her favorite color, pink.
Violet loves studying and learning new things. She is a fan of classical music and dreams of becoming a famouse violinist someday.

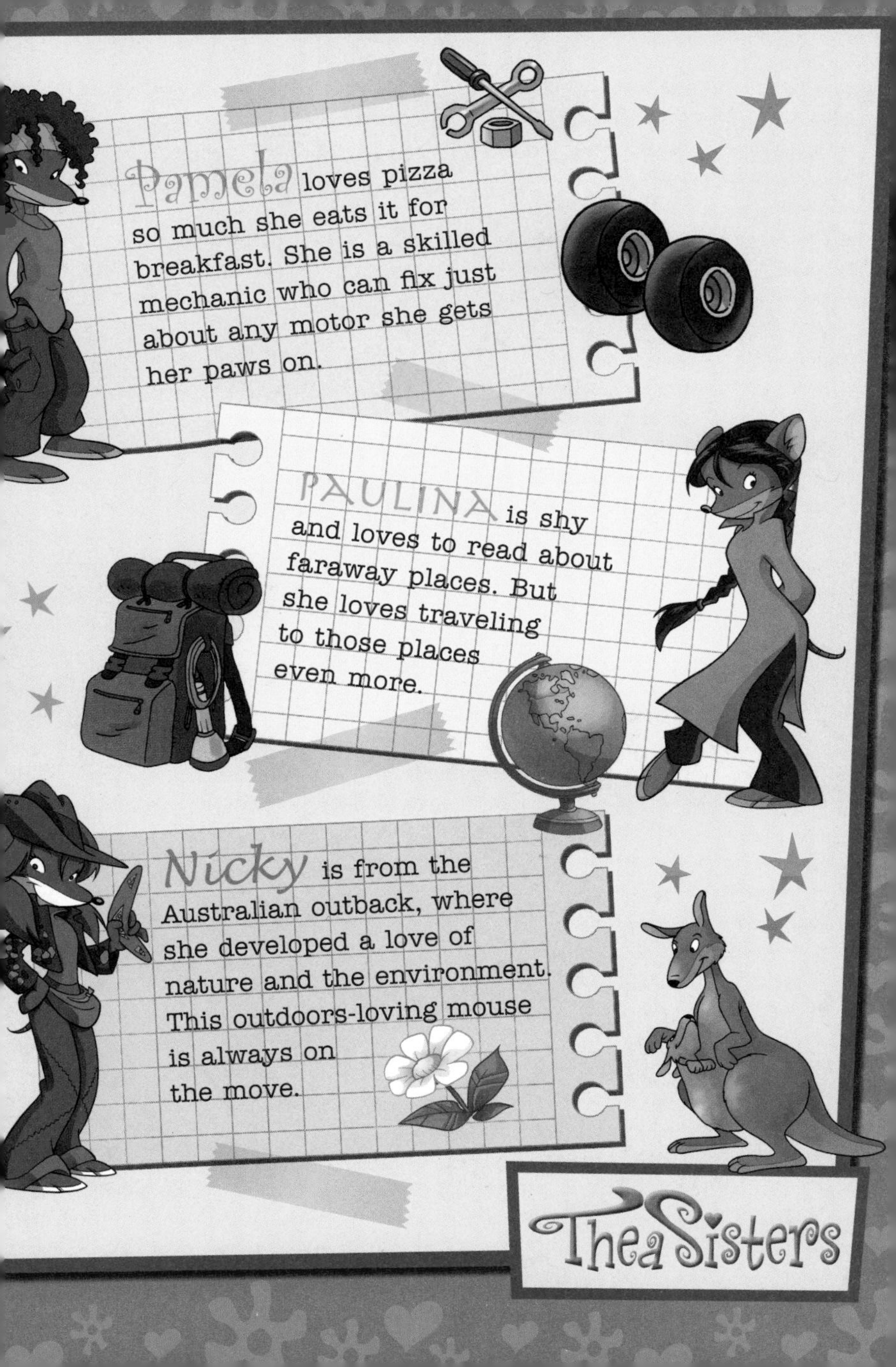
Pamela loves pizza so much she eats it for breakfast. She is a skilled mechanic who can fix just about any motor she gets her paws on.
PAULINA is shy and loves to read about faraway places. But she loves traveling to those places even more.
Nicky is from the Australian outback, where she developed a love of nature and the environment. This outdoors-loving mouse is always on the move.
Thea Sisters

Thea Stilton

MOUSEFORD ACADEMY

THE MISSING DIARY

SWEETWATER COUNTY LIBRARY
Sweetwater County Library System
Green River, WY

Scholastic Inc.

If you purchased this book without a cover, you should be aware that this book is stolen property. It was reported as "unsold and destroyed" to the publisher, and neither the author nor the publisher has received any payment for this "stripped book."

No part of this publication may be reproduced, stored in a retrieval system, or transmitted in any form or by any means, electronic, mechanical, photocopying, recording, or otherwise, without written permission from the copyright holder. For information regarding permission, please contact: Atlantyca S.p.A., Via Leopardi 8, 20123 Milan, Italy; e-mail foreignrights@atlantyca.it, www.atlantyca.com

ISBN 978-0-545-64533-1

Copyright © 2009 by Edizioni Piemme S.p.A., Corso Como 15, 20154 Milan, Italy.

International Rights © Atlantyca S.p.A.

English translation © 2014 by Atlantyca S.p.A.

GERONIMO STILTON and THEA STILTON names, characters, and related indicia are copyright, trademark, and exclusive license of Atlantyca S.p.A. All rights reserved. The moral right of the author has been asserted.

Based on an original idea by Elisabetta Dami.

www.geronimostilton.com

Published by Scholastic Inc., 557 Broadway, New York, NY 10012.
SCHOLASTIC and associated logos are trademarks and/or registered trademarks of Scholastic Inc.

Stilton is the name of a famous English cheese. It is a registered trademark of the Stilton Cheese Makers' Association. For more information, go to www.stiltoncheese.com.

Text by Thea Stilton
Original title *Il diario segreto di Colette*
Cover by Giuseppe Facciotto
Illustrations by Barbara Pellizzari (inks) and Davide Turotti (color)
Graphics by Yuko Egusa

Special thanks to Beth Dunfey
Translated by Lidia Morson Tramontozzi
Interior design by Theresa Venezia

12 11 10 9 18 19/0

Printed in the U.S.A. 40
First printing, January 2014

SPRING FEVER STRIKES AT MOUSEFORD!

After a cold and rainy winter, spring had finally arrived on Whale Island. All over the Mouseford Academy campus, birds were chirping and flowers were budding.

As for the students, they had a full-blown case of SPRING FEVER! The mouselets in the **LIZARDS** — Mouseford's club for girl mice — were meeting in the garden to plan their spring activities. Their first topic: journalism class!

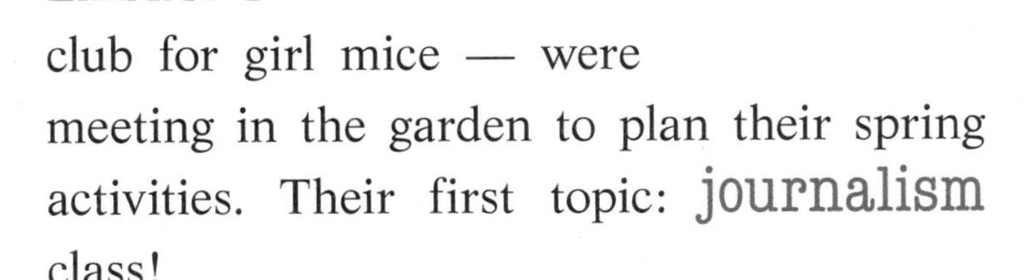

Tanja, the club's president, mentioned the

latest assignment from Professor Rattcliff. The professor had asked her students to publish their own newspaper, and Tanja wanted the Lizards to create a BLOG to go along with it. All the mouselets were excited about the idea.

"When you think about it, every one of us is crazy about a different subject," Tanja pointed out.

"Right!" said Colette enthusiastically.

"So we can each pick a favorite issue to **REPORT** on."

Violet agreed. "Yes! There can be sections on history, current events, new cheeses, fashion, and sports."

"I'll create the website for our blog," offered Paulina, who was a technology EXPERT.

"Of course, we can't do a newspaper without a *gossip* column," said **Ruby Flashyfur**, her eyes gleaming.

Tanja nodded. "Why not? That sounds FUN."

The Thea Sisters — *Colette*, *Nicky*, Pamela, PAULINA, and Violet — weren't so sure. A gossip column sounded like a convenient excuse for spreading **rumors**, and they all knew Ruby loved to make trouble. . . .

LET'S GET TO WORK!

After classes ended the next day, the Lizards set up an old **classroom** as if it were a real newsroom. They washed all the desks and chairs. Then they brought in a few computers for research, blogging, and layouts.

Everyone contributed . . . that is, almost everyone. Ruby didn't lift a paw to help out. She would never dream of cleaning dusty old chairs. Instead, she barked orders at the other mice. "Scrub HARDER! Come on, work those PAWS!"

Ruby and her friends Zoe, Connie, and Alicia made up the Ruby Crew. The four mice didn't think much of the Thea Sisters. In fact, the Ruby Crew acted as

though they were **better** than most of the other students at MOUSEFORD.

Nicky rolled her eyes. "I don't care if she's too LAZY to help, but could she at least stop **squeaking** at us?"

By the end of the afternoon, the newsroom was ready to go! The space was tidy, and Professor Octavius de Mousus, Mouseford's **headmaster**, had agreed to pay to print the paper. Now the only thing the **LIZARDS** needed to do was WRITE!

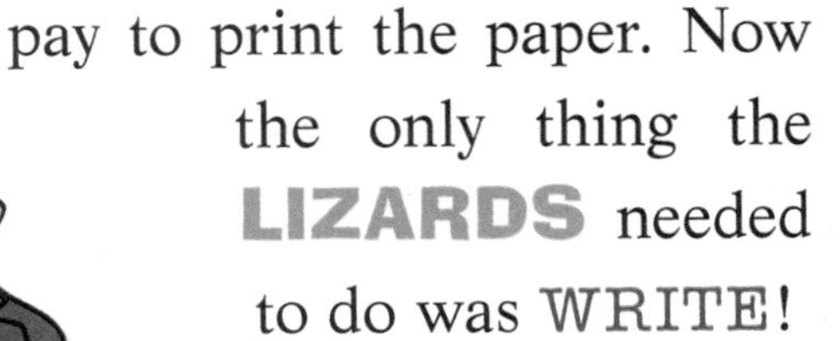

KICKOFF MEETING

The following evening, the Lizards got together for their first **editorial** meeting. The mouselets had been brainstorming ideas between classes, homework, and the daily hubbub of campus life.

Tanja pulled out a *notepad* to keep track of all the story ideas.

Colette was the **first** to squeak up. "I'd like to write an article about this spring's *fashion* trends! Maybe Zoe and I could work **TOGETHER**, since we both keep up with the latest *styles*."

I'll be in char
of fashion

Good for you, Colette!
Oh, how boring!

Zoe shrugged. "I guess, if you want to. . . ."

"Pam and I have been talking about the secrets of Whale Island," Paulina put in. "We want to do a piece about its HIDDEN places."

"Hey, wait a minute," said Connie. "That was *my* idea!"

Pamela smiled at her. "No worries! Why don't we work together, Connie?"

Connie was about to return the smile when a GLARE from Ruby stopped her short.

"The annual **Iron Mouse Games** begin in a few days," Nicky said, "and I wouldn't miss it for all the cheese on Mouse Island! I'd love to write an article about the different **sports** events."

Ruby twirled her tail. "Sports make me snooze!" she complained. "I'll be in charge of the broken hearts column."

Colette, Nicky, Pam, Paulina, and Violet exchanged worried looks. Ruby seemed a little *too* eager to dig up dirt on her classmates. . . .

"Okay, I'll make a note of that," said Tanja, avoiding the Thea Sisters' eyes.

"A newspaper also needs an editor," Tanja continued.

Everyone's eyes turned to her. After all, she was the **PRESIDENT** of the club!

Tanja looked like a mouse caught in a trap. "Er, I know Ruby would be interested. . . ."

"Let's vote by a show of paws," suggested Paulina. "Okay, who wants Ruby as editor?"

Only Ruby, Connie, and Zoe **RAISED** their paws. Alicia raised her paw reluctantly, but only after Zoe tugged her on the tail.

Pam counted. "That's four. How many for Tanja?"

The rest of the Lizards' paws **FLEW** up.

Tanja smiled and bowed. "I'm honored, mouselets! All right, let's meet again in three days. Bring your rough drafts. **Good luck, everyone!**"

As the meeting ended, Ruby tossed her fur.

All right!
Tanja's editor!
Congrats!
Yay!

"Hmpf! All that vote proves is that the mice in this club don't know their Muenster from their mozzarella!"

She scurried up to her room to make a PHONE CALL. "Hello? Mom?"

"Ruby! How are you, my little cheeselet?" Rebecca Flashyfur's squeak was broken up by the crackle of static.

"I need a new camera!" barked Ruby.

Her mother wasn't so sure. "I thought the

one you got for your BIRTHDAY had twenty-two lenses?"

"But I need something more professional!" Ruby whined.

Fifteen minutes later, the Flashyfur **helicopter** flew over Whale Island, dropping off an urgent PACKAGE addressed to Ruby.

A RIVAL PUBLICATION

News of the Lizards' paper spread through the MOUSEFORD campus faster than the smell of melting cheese. When Ruby's brother, Ryder Flashyfur, a member of the **Geckos**, heard about it, he called an emergency meeting in the garden.

"As you know, the **LIZARDS** are creating their own paper," he announced.

They all nodded. No one had squeaked about anything else for days.

"So we **Geckos** must do the same," Ryder continued. "We can't let those mouselets pass us by like yesterday's cheese rinds!"

"Yeah! Let's WRITE our own newspaper," Shen agreed.

Craig, who'd sat down to do a few crunches, wrinkled his snout. "Okay, but I call the **sports** section!"

"**ME, TOO!**" said Marcos.

"I'll take current events," said Shen.

SWEETWATER COUNTY LIBRARY
Sweetwater County Library System
Green River, WY

Let's write our own newspaper!

"You know, the **Iron Mouse Games** are about to begin," said Craig. "We could interview the athletes."

"Great idea," said Ryder. "We'll follow each event, race by race! That can be the theme of our first issue."

"Yeah!" the mice cheered. **"Let's do it!"**

A VERY INTERESTING DIARY

Elsewhere on campus, Nicky, Pamela, Paulina, Violet, and Colette were busy discussing their newspaper articles.

"We've got lots of good ideas," Violet said, "but we'll need more than just ideas to write good stories."

"I just thought of something, mouselets," Colette said. "When Thea was teaching our first journalism class, she gave us loads of advice about putting together a good story. And I jotted it all down in my secret diary!"

"Nice!" Pam said. "But we know your diary is very private. Are you sure you don't mind sharing it with us?"

Colette smiled. "Are you KIDDING me? Of course I don't mind sharing with you. You're like sisters to me. Besides, her advice was meant for all of us. Let me read you a couple of her wisest words. Here we go. . . ."

The Thea Sisters huddled close to Colette and peered over her shoulder. As she turned the diary's PINK pages, the sweet smell of *perfume* filled the air around them.

"Phew!" giggled Nicky. "Colette, this is more than just a diary — it's a fashion statement!"

Colette continued flipping the pages. Anytime she saw one of Thea's tips, she read it **OUT LOUD**.

"'Always remember that an article has to answer six basic questions: Who? What? When? Where? Why? and How?' Oh, here's a good one: 'Treat the rodents you're interviewing *respectfully*.'

"And another one: 'Never be satisfied with just one version of a story. Find out everything you can, and then make sure all the facts are CORRECT.'"

"That's fabumouse advice!" exclaimed Nicky. "You know, I bet we could use the info in Colette's diary to establish ten fundamental **rules** for writing a good news story."

That's fabumouse advice!

"Great idea, Nicky!" said Paulina. "Colette can collect all of **Thea's** advice, and I can post it on the blog for the Lizards to see."

What the mouselets didn't realize was that the **CONTENTS** of Colette's diary were already becoming public! Someone nearby was listening CLOSELY to what the Thea Sisters were reading . . . a bit too closely, in fact!

Ruby was lurking behind a tree with her ears perked up. She was very, *veeeery* interested in Colette's *diary*. . . .

SCOUTING FOR A SCOOP

That afternoon, Ruby went to the Thea Sisters' dorm. Quiet as a mouse, she scurried along the hallway. She was passing almost completely unnoticed when Alicia suddenly poked her snout out of her room. "Ruby! What are you doing here?"

"Sssh!" Ruby hissed. "Keep your squeak down!"

"Sorry!" Alicia whispered. "Now that you're here, though, want to come with me to the harbor? I want to do an article on whales. Feel like shooting a few photos?"

Ruby rolled her eyes. "Uh, no, thanks. I've got a different kind of photo in mind."

Before Alicia could reply, Ruby had turned tail and was peeking inside another student's room. She just knew the dorm would be an endless source of delicious **SCOOPS**!

Sneaking from one hall to another, Ruby **SNAPPED** photos of some really juicy stuff. . . .

First, there was Paulina with a cucumber mask on her snout, photographed through an open door. . . .

Then there was Tanja, who always bragged about her naturally curly fur. Ruby caught her wearing rows and rows of curlers. . . .

And there was Elly Squid playing dress-up in a fancy outfit she'd worn to a costume party on New Year's Eve. . . .

Plus much, much more!

Ruby drew closer and closer to Colette and Pamela's room. And her PAW left its mark wherever she went!

A beauty mask?!
So much for naturally curly fur!
Getting a little old for dress-up, aren't we, Elly?!

Best friends
forever . . . NOT!
Just friends . . .
. . . or secret crushes?!

As Ruby approached Colette's room, Colette flung open the door and ran into Violet and Tanja's room, which was next door. "Hey, Vi, did I leave my FURBRUSH in here?"

Colette had left her door ajar. Ruby took the opportunity to slip inside Colette's room.

And there was the precious *diary*, right on top of Colette's desk! Ruby couldn't believe her good luck. She snatched it up and **darted** out into the hallway again.

COLETTE'S SECRETS

As soon as she got back to the room she shared with Connie, Ruby locked the door behind her. Then she **dove** into Colette's diary. Every few minutes or so, she let out a satisfied snicker.

When Connie tried to get into the room, she found it **locked**. She knocked and knocked before Ruby finally heard her.

"Ruby, it's Zoe and me!" Connie squeaked. "Open up!"

Ruby was so engrossed that she just **GROWLED**, "I'm busy! Give me a minute."

A few minutes later, she opened the door ever so slightly — just wide enough for her FRIENDS to slip in.

"Why didn't you open the door right away?!" asked Connie.

Ruby cautiously stuck her snout out the door and GLANCED up and down the hall. "I found something really interesting," she whispered. She waved the diary under their noses. "This stuff is HOT, mouselets!"

She showed Connie and Zoe a few pages. "Hee, hee, read what she says about her dear friend Pam: 'I waited for Pam in the library for a whole hour, and she never showed up! I was madder than a cat with a bad case of fleas! It made me want to . . . '"

"Well? What does she say then?" asked Connie breathlessly.

Ruby WINKED.

"Maybe we'd better use our imaginations, okay?"

Zoe nodded. She had a mischievous glint in her eyes.

"It's all here, PINK on white," said Ruby.

Listen to what she
wrote here. . . .

She pointed out other excerpts to her friends. "Here she talks about Thea Stilton! And look what she says about Violet! Check out this . . . and this. . . ."

Connie's and Zoe's eyes shone with curiosity.

"I just need to make a couple of changes, and we'll have an article to die for. Wait and see!" Ruby ended triumphantly.

"Squeaking of articles, Zoe, there's something else we need to tell you," said Connie. "I still can't believe Pam and Paulina SWIPED my story idea. But Ruby and I came up with another idea for how to get back at the Thea Sisters!" She motioned to Zoe to come close and started telling her all about their NEFARIOUS plan. . . .

Just because Julie's my older cousin doesn't mean she's my boss!

Wait till I tell Pam what I heard the other mouselets saying. . . .

Violet just doesn't understand that sometimes . . .

A SLIPPERY THIEF!

Meanwhile, Colette had returned to her room. She wanted to finish picking out Thea's tips for her friends. But her diary wasn't on the desk, where she'd left it. WHERE COULD IT BE?

Colette began searching the room. She RUMMAGED around under her desk, between the books, and even under her bed. There was no TRACE of her diary.

"I'm sure it was here before I left the room," she mumbled.

Suddenly, Colette STOPPED. She looked at the door, and then back at her desk. In that moment, she understood everything!

"Oh nooooo! Some slimy sewer rat came in and STOLE it!"

Where's my diary?

Violet scurried into the room.

"Huh? Who stole what, Colette?"

"My diary!" Colette answered miserably. "It's missing. I can't believe it."

"What?!" Violet replied. "Are you sure?"

"Yes, I'm **POSITIVE**," Colette moaned.

Violet called to Nicky, Pam, and Paulina, and they scampered in right away.

Did you look everywhere?

The mouselets searched every nook and cranny in the room AGAIN. But the diary seemed to have VANISHED into thin air!

Colette paced up and down the room like a hungry CAT outside a mousehole.

Violet tried to COMFORT her. "Calm down, Colette. You're wound up tighter than a spring on a mousetrap! What you need is a nice, SOOTHING cup of tea."

A few minutes later, Colette tried to reconstruct what had happened. "I was only gone from the room for a few minutes."

Pamela put her paws on her hips. "Sisters, this is serious! Was there anything EMBARRASSING in the diary?"

Colette shook her snout, getting more and more agitated.

"Of course not," she began. "But I did write all my innermost thoughts, my notes from Thea's lectures, descriptions of all our ADVENTURES . . . everything that was important in my life!"

"Who would do such a *mean* thing?!" Pamela wondered aloud.

"I don't know, but we're going to find out," Nicky declared.

"So who would want to know your life's secrets?" asked Paulina thoughtfully.

There was a moment of SILENCE. Then Pam squeaked up.

"There's a rodent we all know . . ." she began.

". . . who's very interested in other people's secrets . . ." continued Violet.

". . . and who wouldn't miss a chance to play a **dirty trick**. . . ." said Paulina.

"Of course it's . . ." Nicky began.

". . . **Ruby Flashyfur**!" finished Colette.

Who would do such
a mean thing?

Meanwhile, **NIGHT** had fallen. All the lights in the dorm went out one by one. Every light, that is, except the light in Ruby and Connie's room, where Ruby and her friends were still reading the ***STOLEN*** diary.

"**Yaaawn!** She's more long-winded than my great-aunt Chatty McBabblemouse." Connie sighed.

"Uh-huh. And that suits me just fine!" cackled Ruby. She was pleased as Parmesan with the **treasure** she held in her paws.

Connie shot her a funny look. "It's late, Ruby. I'm going to bed."

"No, don't turn off the **light**!" Ruby said sharply. "I want to keep reading."

THE CLOCK'S TICKING!

The Thea Sisters stayed up **LATE**, too. They were busy forming a plan of action. After a few hours' discussion, they decided not to tell anyone about the ***THEFT***, at least for the time being. It was a personal matter, so they agreed they'd FIGURE it out on their own.

The next morning, the mouselets woke up at the crack of **dawn**. The deadline for their newspaper **articles** was looming. The diary's theft couldn't have come at a worse time — they had just a few **hours** to write their articles.

"**Snouts up**, mouselets!" Nicky said. "We'll get Colette's diary back *and* research our stories. It's going to be okay. Remember what Thea always says — friends together, mice forever!"

Then she added, "In the meantime, wish me luck. . . . I'm heading over to the Iron Mouse Games."

"Go, Nicky!" said Paulina, smiling. "You're our favorite SPORTSWRITER!"

REPORTING FROM THE SIDELINES

Elly and Violet decided to join Nicky at the Iron Mouse Games.

"I'd love to get Nina Mousebury's *autograph*," Elly told her friends as they scampered toward the stadium.

"Mousebury is a real champion at the triple **JUMP**," Nicky agreed. "But my favorite event is the four-hundred-meter dash. The FAMOUSE Jesse Rattens will be there!"

"Nina Mousebury? Jesse Rattens?" echoed Craig, who was leaving campus with Shen and Ryder. "Are you going to the Iron Mouse Games?"

"Yeah!" said Nicky **CHEERFULLY**. "Are you going, too?"

Shen nodded, blushing a little. "We're doing research for a class project."

"Oh, really?" said Violet. "So are we! The **LIZARDS** are putting together a newspaper for Professor Rattcliff's journalism class."

"That's also what we're doing," Craig admitted. "We're writing articles for the first issue of the **Geckos**' new newspaper. It's a special edition that we're calling *The Sportsmouse*!"

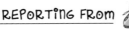

t put the cheese
before the
cracker!

Elly, Nicky, and Violet looked at one another in surprise. **TWO NEWSPAPERS?**

Everyone was silent for a moment. Then Violet squeaked up. "Well, since we're all here for the same reason, why don't we work **together**?"

"Sure!" said Shen. He considered the Thea Sisters good friends.

Craig gave Shen a not-so-subtle nudge. "Don't put the cheese before the cracker!" he said. "We've got to take a vote first."

"Well, I think it's a **GREAT** idea. Let's do it," said Ryder.

Nicky smiled. "Okay, then, we're a team! At least for this story."

Outside the **STADIUM**, the young reporters divided up assignments.

Craig and Nicky would follow the **track** races, Violet and Ryder the **JUMPING** events, and Elly and Shen would report on everything else.

When they explained to the stadium's organizers that they were there as journalists, they got permission to go onto

the field's sidelines to interview the athletes and take photographs.

"Wow! I've never seen a race this close before!" said Craig. He was in awe. "I can't believe we're right on the SIDELINES!"

"It's an amazing opportunity," Nicky agreed. At that moment, the fans' CHEERING grew louder. "Come on, let's HAUL TAIL! The first race is about to begin."

Nicky and Craig scurried off.

A SUSPICIOUS FINISH

By the time Nicky and Craig found a spot on the sidelines, the runners in the 400-meter dash were already WARMING up.

Nicky kept an eye on the track through her camera's powerful lens. She was checking out the judges, who were busy with last-minute preparations. That's when she noticed one judge near the photocell* at the finish line.

Nicky **zoomed** in as the judge peered over his shoulder. He was fumbling with the photocell.

"Hey, Craig," she hissed. "**LOOK!** There's something funny going on at the finish line."

"Oh, I wouldn't worry," Craig reassured her. "Everything here's on the up-and-up. Let's get our cameras ready — the

* A photocell is used in athletic competitions to show who placed first, second, third, etc.

semifinalists are about to take off!"

At that moment, they heard the shot signaling the beginning of the race. With a jolt, the athletes sprinted from the starting blocks.

The stadium's commentator was analyzing the event over the loudsqueaker. His remarks grew more and more COLORFUL.

"And they're out of the gate! There's a tight

Rattens sprints!
Rattens pulls ahead!
Rattens . . .

crowd at the head of the pack. But here comes the **favorite**, Jesse Rattens! He's pulling into the LEAD. Oh, wait . . . now he's going snout-to-snout with Joe Swifterson!"

The entire stadium watched as the two mice CROSSED the finish line.

"**INCREDIBLE!**" the commentator cried. "What a tight race! It looked like

Rattens won, but the photo finish shows Joe Swifterson as the winner!"

The stadium shook with the fans' **roars** of disbelief.

The commentator was silent for a moment.

"That's right!" he continued. "Swifterson came in first and Rattens second. Next up, the final ***RACE***!"

Nicky frowned. "Something smells fishier than day-old tuna," she murmured.

Craig's snout darkened. "That is really bizarre. . . . Rattens is phenomenal at ***sprints***! Swifterson, on the other paw, is famouse for slowing down at the finish line."

"But Swifterson's sponsor is **super-rich** and very ambitious!" Nicky put in. "Let's keep a close **EYE** on the finals. I have a FUNNY feeling about this."

TIME FOR TEAMWORK

Between events, Nicky, Violet, Elly, Craig, and Ryder gathered high in the stands. They were **worried** about what they'd just witnessed.

"What are we going to do?" asked Elly.

Nicky wasn't sure. "I don't have a plan yet. Let's put our snouts **together**. One of us is bound to come up with an **idea**."

Shen thought for a bit. "We need to keep an eye on the entire track. But let's not forget Nicky's **suspicions**. We've got to pay the most attention to the finish line."

"I'll do it," offered Craig. "I'll find a spot right behind the judge, and I won't let him out of my **SIGHT**!"

Nicky placed a paw on his shoulder. "Be careful," she warned. "I'm not sure that's the best plan. If the judge feels he's being WATCHED, he'll be more cautious, and then we won't have any proof."

She considered for a minute. "I've got an idea," Nicky continued. "Craig, your camera has the most powerful lens. You

can watch the finish line from a safe distance, where no one will notice you."

"Good idea, Nick," said Violet. "Take a look at this. I made a **sketch** of the stadium and marked the best places to observe the action."

The friends quickly split up and went to the positions Violet had MARKED in her diagram. Violet planted herself near the starting blocks; Shen stationed himself in the middle of the track; Nicky and Elly stood by the finish line; and Ryder and Craig stood on the sidelines, ready to photograph anything and everything.

There was a loud shot, and the final race **began**! Violet gave Shen a paws-up sign. So far, the judges had stuck to the rules.

Shen watched the athletes **SPRINT** off and raised a paw: That meant everything was going **smoothly**.

At the end of the race, the photo finish again showed that Swifterson was the winner.

But Nicky had been watching closely, and she had her own opinion on the matter: Rattens had crossed the finish line first! A **FRAME** from her digital camera proved she was right.

While the fans halfheartedly **applauded** Swifterson, the Mouseford friends gathered under the bleachers.

1
The runners in the starting blocks, ready to sprint!
2
The athletes halfway around the track.

1
The runners approach the finish line, where a judge furtively moves the photocell.
1
4
Swifterson and Rattens are snout-to-snout, but Rattens gets to the finish line first!

Nicky showed her friends the picture. "Look here, everyone. You can see it perfectly. Rattens put his paw on the finish line first!"

Craig SMILED as he showed the photo he'd taken from above. "I shot a complete sequence of frames. Check this out. The judge is moving the photocell to give Swifterson the victory!"

"Great job, Craig!" cried Nicky. The two friends high-fived. Violet was beside herself with excitement. "What a SCOOP! And we did it with teamwork."

"Absolutely," said Ryder. "We've got to warn the race officials. We've got proof of the SCAM!"

Thanks to the students' photographs, the

fraud was REVEALED.

And the story got even more dramatic when the dishonest judge was dismissed! A team of security rats escorted him from the stadium.

A few minutes later, Jesse Rattens climbed to the HIGHEST step on the podium to receive his gold medal. His fans cheered wildly.

Craig grinned with satisfaction. "I knew Rattens was the best!"

Meanwhile, back at Mouseford Academy, a very different kind of trick was under way. . . .

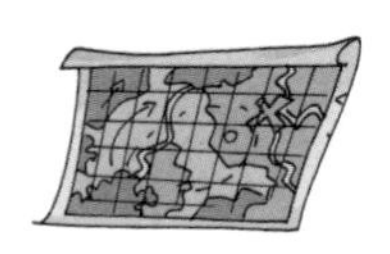

PACKED AND READY TO GO!

"Are you ready yet? Can we get going?" Pam was waiting impatiently in front of the Academy. She had a huge backpack in one paw and the keys to her SUV in the other.

"Here I am," Paulina said BREATHLESSLY as she scurried up to her friend. "Let's hope Connie doesn't pull one of her tricks."

Pam winked. "Who knows, maybe this trip will prove she's not so bad after all!"

Paulina was skeptical. "That would be a pleasant surprise."

The three mouselets were headed for RAM PLAIN, a valley rich in FOSSILS.

The fossils lay at the foot of a very high

peak. According to geologists, their presence showed that Whale Island was once completely submerged in WATER. It was the perfect place for Connie, Pam, and Paulina to research their article about the island's history.

Pamela and Paulina left CAMPUS and found Connie waiting by the SUV. She was carrying a little backpack and a HUGE canvas bag.

Pam scrambled behind the wheel, and Paulina climbed up front next to her. Connie got settled in the back and pulled two envelopes out of her bag. "I took care of everything we'll need. I got each of us a trail map that'll take us to Ram Plain, a compass, and a summary of the history of Whale Island."

Pamela looked at the envelope in

FORD
EMY
Let's go, mouselets!

surprise. "Wow! That's so NICE of you, Connie."

"Yeah, thanks, Connie!" said Paulina.

Connie shrugged. "No skin off my cheese. But we'd better get going. It's getting LATE!"

Pamela steered the SUV onto a dirt road, which soon turned into a narrow PATH that took them deep into the WOODS. About twenty minutes later, they'd arrived.

As soon as she climbed out of the SUV, Connie smacked her snout. "Oh no, I'm such a cheesebrain!"

Paulina and Pam looked at her CURIOUSLY. "What's wrong?"

"I forgot my MOUSEPAD!" Connie cried.

Paulina thrust a paw inside her backpack. "No problem, you can use mine."

Connie stared at her icily. "Oh, that's so sweet of you! But I'm afraid I can't just use any old MousePad. I need mine. It's an exclusive model — very HIGH-TECH."

Pam and Paulina offered to drive her back to the Academy, but Connie shook her snout. "No way. If we all go BACK, we'll lose too much time."

"But if you go and come back alone, that'll take even longer," Paulina pointed out.

"I'll walk to the Academy and then drive back in my CAR," Connie said. "I can't possibly do without my MousePad! You go on and I'll catch up."

Pamela and Paulina looked at each other and shrugged. They headed toward the woods as Connie scampered off in the OPPOSITE direction.

As soon as Pam and Paulina were out of sight, Connie laughed to herself. "Go ahead, mouselets! I've planned a nice little surprise for you. . . ."

LOST IN THE WOODS

Half an hour later, Pam and Paulina were deep in the woods.

"Hmm . . . isn't this way NORTH?" Pam asked, looking at her compass in confusion.

Paulina scratched her snout. "Impossible! The sun is over there and the moss is growing on this side of the rocks."

Pam shook the compass and then threw up her paws. "I don't know what to think."

The mouselets turned to their maps. "Something's not right," said Paulina. "According to this, there should be a lake right under our tails!"

The friends exchanged a look of concern.

"What do we do?" Paulina asked.

"Well, I'm not going to stand here and let

the grass grow beneath my paws!" Pam exclaimed. "Let's head toward the valley. Then we'll figure out how to get back to Mouseford."

They trudged along a path that was barely **VISIBLE** in the dense forest. The farther

they walked, the thicker the **BRANCHES** and underbrush became. The light of the sun filtered feebly through the tree limbs. It grew cooler in the shade. And the ground became very **slippery**! Suddenly . . .

WHOOOOOSHHHHHHHH!

The tranquil afternoon was shattered by the sound of paws crashing down, down, down.

"EEEEEEEK!"

Paulina whirled around. "Pam? Pam, where are you? Paaaaaam?!?"

A tiny, faraway squeak answered her. "Paulina, I'm down here!"

Paulina hurried to the place where Pamela had been a moment before. Her friend had tumbled into a ditch!

"Are you okay?"

"Yeah, yeah, I'm all right. Just a couple of SCRATCHES."

Pam began to look around her. Where was she? She scraped her paw against the ground, moving leaves, rocks, and dirt.

"Can you make it back up?" shouted Paulina. Her friend's squeak sounded so far away.

"Paulina, I'm not even remotely thinking about coming up. Come down and see what I FOUND!" Pam shouted.

Paulina cautiously shimmied **down** the side of the ditch. She couldn't wait to see what her friend had discovered.

MISSING MOUSELETS

Back at the Academy, the **LIZARDS** were about to start reviewing everyone's first drafts. Colette, Nicky, and Violet headed toward the conference room.

"Has anyone seen Pam?" asked Colette.

Nicky shook her snout.

"I haven't seen her or Paulina since last **NIGHT**," said Violet. "When was the last time you heard from them?"

"This morning they were supposed to go to **RAM PLAIN** with Connie," Colette replied.

"I guess we'll catch up with them at the **meeting**," said Nicky.

Each member of the staff took a seat.

"Good to see you, mouselets. Are we all here?" Tanja asked.

Nicky looked around. "PAM and PAULINA aren't here yet. Has anyone seen them?"

"They're probably on their way back from Ram Plain," Connie said, SHRUGGING. "We were supposed to go together, but they didn't wait for me."

Colette, Nicky, and Violet looked at one another in SURPRISE. That didn't sound like Pam and Paulina! Something was definitely **WRONG**.

Tanja changed the subject. "Well, let's get started. First we should take a look at our **drafts**. When Paulina comes in, she can update us on the blog."

The Lizards all took out their *notepads* and began to share their work.

The room began buzzing with busy chatter.

"Read this!"

"Look what I found!"

"What a **SCOOP**!"

"Okay, everyone, one at a time," said Ruby, raising her **squeak**. She banged her notepad on the table to get their attention. "Please, let's start with our lead story. I have **BIG** news to share!"

SPITEFUL STORIES

Once all eyes were on her, Ruby spread a few COLORFUL pages out on the table in front of everyone.

"But, Ruby, you weren't supposed to design the pages!" Tanja said. "You know that! At the first meeting we decided that Paulina would do the graphics and the layout."

"Oh, I'm sorry, I just wanted to **SAVE** her some work," Ruby said sweetly.

The club members began passing Ruby's pages from paw to paw. Everyone MURMURED curiously. A couple of the mouselets turned to look at Colette.

"Colette, what is it?" asked Violet. Colette suddenly turned PALE as mozzarella.

But . . . but . . . these . . .
Colette, what is it?
ANCHOVY ADDICT!
Pee-yew! Who likes stinky fish?
VIOLET JUST DOESN'T UNDERSTAND!
A friendship in crisis!

BEAUTY MASK!?!
More like a monster mask!
CURLY FUR FRAUD!
Modest mouse really vain at heart!

She pointed to one of Ruby's gossip pages.

"Violet, this . . . this is from my diary! Not the way Ruby wrote them here, but close enough. She stole this straight from my diary! Please don't get MAD. . . . Just let me explain!"

Violet was HORRIFIED. But before she could squeak, Ruby tore a page from her notebook and placed it on the table.

"I have another brilliant idea to share. I came up with the idea of writing a short essay on the art of journalism," Ruby explained. "Something simple and CLEAR for everyone to understand. Something I wrote as I looked back on all my experiences," she said confidently.

Nicky and Violet helped Colette out of the chair she had FALLEN into. Quiet as mice, they scampered out of the room.

TEN FUNDAMENTALS OF GOOD JOURNALISM

1. Choose your words carefully.
2. Write brief sentences.
3. Never take anything for granted; explain everything.
4. Always verify the reliability of your sources.
5. Treat the rodents you interview with respect.
6. Try to remain impartial.
7. Leave room for everyone's opinion.

Search for the truth.

NEVER LIE.

Always be curious and never be satisfied.

"Violet, please — I have to tell you . . ." Colette STUTTERED.

Violet put her paw around her friend's shoulder. "Don't worry, Colette. I know you wouldn't say anything BAD about me. It's that Ruby twisting your words!"

Nicky nodded. "You said it, sis. It's time to get the Thea Sisters together. We have to FIND Pam and Paulina! Then we'll figure out what to do about Ruby."

THE RESCUE TEAM!

Soon the whole Mouseford campus was buzzing with the news that Pam and Paulina were missing. Colette, Nicky, and Violet quickly put together a RESCUE team. Paulina's friend Shen was one of the first to volunteer.

Before long, many mouselets had gathered to help. As the sun slowly dipped below the **horizon**, the team began its search.

They traced Pamela's SUV to the spot where it was parked near the edge of the woods. Nicky examined the tracks nearby. "Look, there are three sets of PAW PRINTS here. So there must have been three rodents. One set is headed back toward school. . . ."

"Could it have been Connie?" asked Violet.

"Maybe. The other two sets of prints go into the woods," Nicky replied.

Shen was hopeful. "Those prints must belong to Pamela and Paulina!"

"Then let's go find them!" said Nicky. The group of mice began following the trail their friends had left behind.

After just a few steps, they stopped. "Look! Doesn't that belong to Pam?" Violet cried.

They had found the first clue! Lying on the ground where the path divided was a wrench. It was a marker Pamela and Paulina had placed to help them find their way back.

"Definitely!" agreed Nicky. "Knowing Pam, I'll bet its tip points in the direction they took."

The rodents continued forward in silence. The woods were DARK by now, and it was a little spooky. Colette, Nicky, Violet, and their friends turned on the *flashlights* they had brought with them.

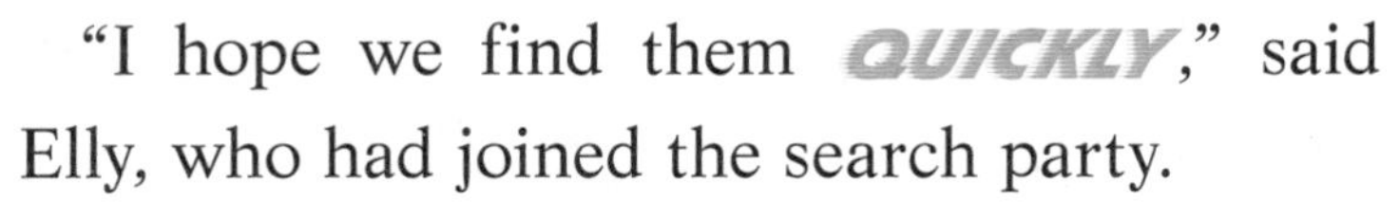

"I hope we find them *QUICKLY*," said Elly, who had joined the search party.

"All we need is a few more **clues**," Colette said.

"And here's one right now!" cried Nicky, aiming her flashlight at a twig with two thin blades of grass TIED around it.

"We always use this CODE when we go hiking," explained Violet. "It means they went in that direction, and then turned right two times. Pam and Paulina left this here to help them find their way back."

A little farther along the path, the team found a few pebbles arranged in the shape of an arrow. They followed the direction of the arrow, and soon spotted an orderly row of STICKS that led to the exact place where Pam had tumbled down!

"Do we have to go down there?" asked Colette in alarm. "It's so STEEP!"

"Don't be afraid, we'll be just fine," said Nicky, trying to reassure her. "I brought ropes just in case. We can use them to pull ourselves back up." She was an excellent climber.

One after the other, everyone slid down the slope.

Paulina and Pamela heard their friends arrive and ran to them.

"THANK GOODMOUSE you're here!" said Paulina.

"We've been waiting for you," said Pam. "We knew you'd come!"

"And we knew you two wouldn't be a bit frightened by a little ADVENTURE like this!" said Nicky.

"Frightened?" answered Pamela. "More like fired up! Come see what we found."

A FABUMOUSE DISCOVERY!

Pamela and Paulina took their friends by the paw and led them to the mouth of a mysterious CAVE. "We're almost positive this cave has never been discovered," Paulina said.

Pamela took a few steps inside. "We didn't have the proper equipment to explore it. We only had our flashlights . . . but look what you can see from here!"

The group took a few more cautious steps forward. Paulina shone the flashlight on an enormouse stalactite that was slowly dripping water. A little stream, very clear and gurgling, flowed beneath it.

"Look underneath the water's surface. See

those little rocks there?” Pam asked.

Everyone moved nearer to the stream to take a better look. The little stones looked like gravel, but more transparent. They were perfectly shaped, like tiny globes.

“These are cave pearls!” Paulina explained. “Little DROPS of water and limestone fall from the stalactite into the stream. Bit by bit, the current molds the limestone into ROUND pebbles. It takes thousands of years to create these pearls!”

The group gazed in silence at those perfectly smooth globes nature had so patiently formed.

“Mouselets, this is a real find!“ Nicky exclaimed. “WHAT A SCOOP!”

What a scoop!

"And all the credit goes to Connie!" said Paulina, giggling.

Elly frowned. "What do you mean?"

Pamela showed her the back of her compass. "Look at this. She stuck small MAGNETS under the compasses she gave us. The magnets interfered with the needle and made us get lost!"

"And that's not all," said Paulina. "She gave us the wrong map, too! After all that work she did to fake the map . . ."

". . . she ended up doing you a favor!" Shen said, laughing.

Excited about their unexpected discovery, the group climbed out of the ditch and hurried back to the Academy as quickly as their paws could carry them.

THE HOUR OF RECKONING

"Mouselets, I promise . . . I had nothing to do with it!" Connie protested. Pamela and Paulina had **cornered** her at the entrance to the library.

Paulina frowned. "Connie, you owe us an EXPLANATION."

I have no idea what happened. . . .

But Connie just made excuses. "I downloaded the maps from the Internet. Maybe there was a printer ERROR."

Paulina put her paws on her hips. "Uh-huh. And what about the compasses?!"

"Oh, the compasses . . . Were yours ACTING UP, too? I got lost, and I had a hard time finding the right way. By the time I got to Ram Plain, it was so late I was sure you had already left."

Paulina twisted her whiskers skeptically. She was not a bit convinced.

"Your story has more holes in it than a slice of SWISS, Connie," Pam said. "Why don't you just admit what you did? Don't you owe it to us to be honest?"

Connie rolled her eyes. "But I didn't do ANYTHING! Really! In fact, I feel just TERRIBLE about what happened to you. . . ."

Pamela and Paulina sighed.

There was no way to make her tell the truth. They shrugged and went into the library.

Zoe scampered up to Connie. "You did the right thing. DENY everything!" she whispered. "Besides, they don't have any proof!"

"Yeah, it turns out I was the one who was conned," replied Connie acidly. "**Luck** was on their side! I should have been the one to find that cave."

Inside the library, Pam began to download the photos she'd taken inside the cave. Paulina settled near her and scanned their article into the Lizards' newly created blog.

One after another, the Lizards filed in and pawed Paulina their articles for layout.

Elly came first. "Paulina, I emailed you my article on the history of the port."

Then Zoe and Colette gave her their article. "Here! These are the photos we chose for the fashion column."

Soon, Paulina was wading through page after page of text and photos. When Shen passed by carrying a stack of heavy BOOKS, he hit the corner of the table where Paulina was working. His books tumbled onto the table, knocking the stack of articles to the ground!

"Oops!" exclaimed Paulina. She bent to

pick up her papers as Shen apologized.

Under the table, something caught her eye.

The corner of a pink notebook was peeking out of the top of a duffel bag. It looked exactly like Colette's diary!

Paulina glanced up to identify the bag's owner. It was Ruby Flashyfur! She was completely engrossed in typing her article.

Paulina knew she had to get the diary back. It was now or never! But how?

THE TRUTH COMES OUT

Paulina scrambled to her paws and whispered something in Shen's ear. A moment later, Shen stood up casually. As he passed by Ruby, he pretended to **TRIP** over her bag. (In fact, he gave it a well-aimed KICK!)

The contents of the bag immediately spilled all over the floor.

"Watch where you put your paws, you CLUMSY cheddarface!" snapped Ruby, bending to pick up her things.

A squeak behind Ruby nearly made her jump out of her fur.

"Excuse me, Ruby, but what is my diary doing in your bag?"

It was Colette!

Ruby's big **GREEN EYES** widened in surprise. "What?! I don't know anything about it. Somebody must have put it there!"

The other Thea Sisters surrounded her and looked at her **sternly**.

Very **calmly**, Colette reached down and picked up her diary. "You know, Ruby, I'll bet a few passages from my diary might clear up some things. . . ."

Curious to know what was going on, the other students in the library **gathered** around the little group.

Ruby shrugged. "I don't know why you'd think I care about your *stupid diary*. . . ."

"Oh, is that so?" said Colette. "Well then, let's see if any of this sounds familiar: Pam is totally obsessed with anchovy pizza! Wait till I tell her what I heard the other mouselets saying. . . . There's a new pizza shop on the corner, and they serve three different kinds of anchovy pizza. She's going to be thrilled! And here's another one: Violet just doesn't UNDERSTAND . . . that sometimes a nice pawicure calms me down twice as fast as a cup of herbal tea!"

Colette looked at Ruby **defiantly**. "Hmm, that reminds me of something . . . your gossip column! But it doesn't quite match your version of events, does it, Ruby?"

With everyone **STARING** at her, Ruby was struck squeakless. The other members of the Ruby Crew were too embarrassed to defend her.

Colette was determined to get everything out in the open. "Oh, wait, look what else is in here. Some tips about **writing a good news story**! Ruby, if you're going to copy Thea Stilton, at least quote her correctly!"

A buzz of indignant MURMURS rose from her audience. From the other side of the

room, Professor Rattcliff came forward.

"Miss Flashyfur, I couldn't help but overhear everything. This is unacceptable behavior for an aspiring journalist, and for a student at this school! I must squeak with the **headmaster** about this immediately."

Before Ruby could reply, Professor Rattcliff strode away.

THERE'S A LESSON IN THIS!

News about what had happened in the library traveled across campus faster than a hyperactive hamster on a treadmill. No one SQUEAKED about anything else all day.

That evening, Headmaster Octavius de Mousus called everyone into a **special assembly**. As the students took their seats, they all whispered to one another. Many of them pointed at Ruby.

A few minutes later, the headmaster and several *professors* filed in. The teachers looked very serious and solemn.

The students' chattering stopped at once. The headmaster sat at a podium and began to squeak.

We have to do something!

"Students, we have called you here today because something **serious** happened at this institution. One of our students has behaved **DISHONESTLY**, and has broken Mouseford Academy's sacred honor code."

All eyes turned to Ruby, who looked indifferent. The other mouselets from her crew, who were sitting nearby, **SHIFTED** uncomfortably in their seats.

"In this case, the **rules** of privacy and good journalism have been violated," the headmaster continued. "I'm very sorry for what has happened, but I believe that for every mistake, there's also an opportunity to **LEARN**."

The students held their breath, waiting to hear what Professor de Mousus would say next.

"I am planning to **punish** the student who made this mistake. But I also want all of you to learn from her error so none of you will ever make the same mistake. Today we're holding a special session on good journalism. We've invited an exceptional teacher to help us. I'm pleased to introduce you all to one of Mouse Island's most distinguished journalists, **Thea Stilton**!"

A loud round of applause greeted Thea's entrance. As she took her place in front of the microphone, she **winked** at the five mouselets seated in the first row.

All the students whipped out notebooks and PENS from their backpacks. They wanted to be ready to record every word Thea said.

Thea's speech was simple, clear, and to the point — just like a good article! Even Ruby was taking notes.

"A reporter's job is a fabumouse one," Thea began. "A good journalist must be curious to learn about everything around her, and unafraid to ask questions. Most important, she has to be HONEST and tell what she has discovered in the simplest words possible! Anyone who lies, falsifies a statement, or plays with the truth is not a journalist. In fact, she or he is a rodent who should not be trusted."

The Thea Sisters nodded in agreement.

"My advice to students interested in

journalism is this: Don't compete with one another. Instead, practice **collaboration**. Work together and help one another.

"That way, everyone has a chance to learn. Sharing information will help reveal the **truth**!"

There was a hearty round of **applause**.

When Thea was done, Ryder got up and asked to squeak. Everyone was surprised — no one knew what he was going to say.

Ryder cleared his throat. "The Geckos and Lizards worked well together when we covered the Iron Mouse Games. We propose the two clubs **JOIN FORCES** to publish one paper:

THE OFFICIAL MOUSEFORD ACADEMY NEWSPAPER!"

The walls shook with enthusiastic cheers at this proposal.

HOORAY! HOORAY! HOORAY!

Colette, Nicky, Pam, Paulina, Violet, and Tanja looked at one another and smiled.

"Okay, let's do it!" said Nicky.

Thea SMILED approvingly. "I love it when a great team comes together. That's what teamwork is all about!"

Don't miss these exciting Thea Sisters adventures!

Thea Stilton and the Dragon's Code

Thea Stilton and the Mountain of Fire

Thea Stilton and the Ghost of the Shipwreck

Thea Stilton a
Secret Ci

Thea Stilton and the Mystery in Paris

Thea Stilton and the Cherry Blossom Adventure

Thea Stilton and the Star Castaways

Thea Stilton: Big Trouble in the Big Apple

Thea Stilton a
Ice Treasu

Thea Stilton and the Secret of the Old Castle

Thea Stilton and the Blue Scarab Hunt

Thea Stilton and the Prince's Emerald

Thea Stilton and the Mystery on the Orient Express

Thea Stilton a
Dancing Sha

Thea Stilton and the Legend of the Fire Flowers

Thea Stilton and the Spanish Dance Mission

Thea Stilton and the Journey to the Lion's Den

Thea Stilton and the Great Tulip Heist

Thea Stilton a
Chocolate Sal

Be sure to read all my fabumouse adventures!

1 Lost Treasure of
the Emerald Eye

#2 The Curse of the
Cheese Pyramid

#3 Cat and Mouse in a
Haunted House

#4 I'm Too Fond of
My Fur!

#5 Four Mice Deep in
the Jungle

#6 Paws Off,
Cheddarface!

#7 Red Pizzas for a
Blue Count

#8 Attack of the
Bandit Cats

#9 A Fabumouse
Vacation for Geronimo

#10 All Because of a
Cup of Coffee

11 It's Halloween,
ou 'Fraidy Mouse!

#12 Merry Christmas,
Geronimo!

#13 The Phantom of
the Subway

#14 The Temple of the
Ruby of Fire

#15 The Mona Mousa
Code

6 A Cheese-Colored
Camper

#17 Watch Your
Whiskers, Stilton!

#18 Shipwreck on the
Pirate Islands

#19 My Name Is Stilton,
Geronimo Stilton

#20 Surf's Up,
Geronimo!

#21 The Wild, Wild West

#22 The Secret of Cacklefur Castle

A Christmas Tale

#23 Valentine's Day Disaster

#24 Field Trip
Niagara Falls

#25 The Search for Sunken Treasure

#26 The Mummy with No Name

#27 The Christmas Toy Factory

#28 Wedding Crasher

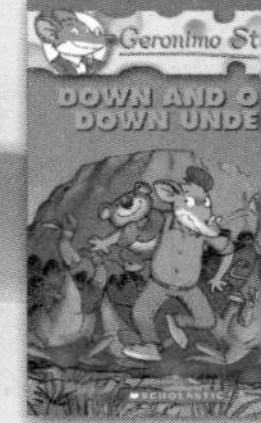

#29 Down and
Down Under

#30 The Mouse Island Marathon

#31 The Mysterious Cheese Thief

Christmas Catastrophe

#32 Valley of the Giant Skeletons

#33 Geronimo an
Gold Medal Myst

#34 Geronimo Stilton, Secret Agent

#35 A Very Merry Christmas

#36 Geronimo's Valentine

#37 The Race Across America

#38 A Fabumou
School Adventu

#39 Singing Sensation

#40 The Karate Mouse

#41 Mighty Mount Kilimanjaro

#42 The Peculiar Pumpkin Thief

#43 I'm Not
Supermouse!

#44 The Giant
iamond Robbery

#45 Save the White
Whale!

#46 The Haunted
Castle

#47 Run for the Hills,
Geronimo!

#48 The Mystery in
Venice

#49 The Way of
the Samurai

#50 This Hotel Is
Haunted

#51 The Enormouse
Pearl Heist

#52 Mouse in Space!

#53 Rumble in
the Jungle

54 Get into Gear,
Stilton!

#55 The Golden
Statue Plot

#56 Flight of the
Red Bandit

Special
Edition!

The Hunt for the
Golden Book

#57 The Stinky
Cheese Vacation

Don't miss my journey through time!

Mouseford

Teachers' living quarters

Athletic fields

Dorms

Garden

South Tower

Library

HERB GARDEN
NORTH TOWER
DMASTER'S OFFICE
CAFETERIA
GREAT HALL
MOUSEFORD
CLASSROOMS

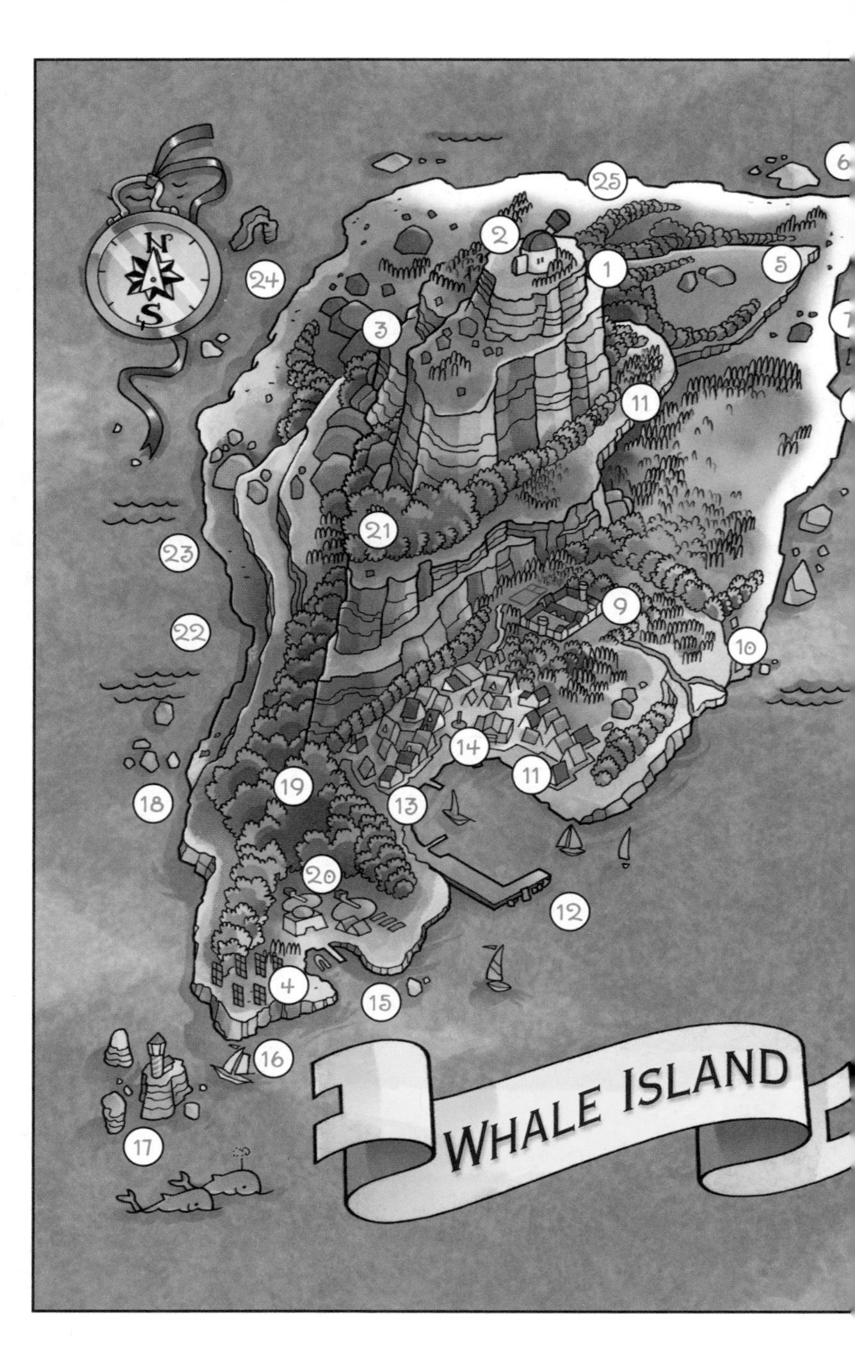
N
S
WHALE ISLAND
1
2
3
4
5
6
9
10
11
11
12
13
14
15
16
17
18
19
20
21
22
23
24
25

MAP OF WHALE ISLAND

1. Falcon Peak
2. Observatory
3. Mount Landslide
4. Solar Energy Plant
5. Ram Plain
6. Very Windy Point
7. Turtle Beach
8. Beachy Beach
9. Mouseford Academy
10. Kneecap River
11. Mariner's Inn
12. Port
13. Squid House
14. Town Square
15. Butterfly Bay
16. Mussel Point
17. Lighthouse Cliff
18. Pelican Cliff
19. Nightingale Woods
20. Marine Biology Lab
21. Hawk Woods
22. Windy Grotto
23. Seal Grotto
24. Seagulls Bay
25. Seashell Beach

THANKS FOR READING,
AND GOOD-BYE UNTIL OUR
NEXT ADVENTURE!

Thea Sisters